City Noir: Crime Stories from Four Corners of India

Mitrajit Biswas

Ukiyoto Publishing

All global publishing rights are held by

Ukiyoto Publishing

Published in 2024

Content Copyright © Mitrajit Biswas

ISBN 9789362693662

All rights reserved.
No part of this publication may be reproduced, transmitted, or stored in a retrieval system, in any form by any means, electronic, mechanical, photocopying, recording or otherwise, without the prior permission of the publisher.

The moral rights of the author have been asserted.

This is a work of fiction. Names, characters, businesses, places, events, locales, and incidents are either the products of the author's imagination or used in a fictitious manner. Any resemblance to actual persons, living or dead, or actual events is purely coincidental.

This book is sold subject to the condition that it shall not by way of trade or otherwise, be lent, resold, hired out or otherwise circulated, without the publisher's prior consent, in any form of binding or cover other than that in which it is published.

www.ukiyoto.com

Contents

Calling 011	1
The glare of lustful eyes	1
Another brick in the wall	4
Knock-Knock who is there?!	8
Corner of Marquis Street	12
The shack at the beach	13
Looking inside the camera lens	15
Operation White Line	18
Bored past sunset	21
Epitaph at Delta Beach	24
Vannakam Chennai	25
Boom and investigative journalism	27
A story beyond a story	30
Pieces of information in a sea of maze	33
Confused and Flummoxed	35
J.N.U. Campus	37
Parsi Cafe	39
The maximum city beckons	40
Krishna the charioteer	43
CST	46
The sling and the shot	50
Let the curtains drop	52
About the Author	**54**

Calling 011

The glare of lustful eyes

The winter had set in, and I had enrolled in the undergraduate course in a university on the outskirts of NCR. The exact location would be Haryana. This was my first experience of coming to a place outside my home city, Kolkata. I had not idea that it would change my life in a manner which I had not expected and make me end up as an investigative journalist. They say everything starts as an accident and as cliched as it sounds it did hold true for me. I was just settling in my university and the winter was definitely chilly and biting. I had joined the program in Journalism. Since early days, I always used to be very much inspired from Tintin comics. The campus was huge and had amazing grounds. However, I had always been much of a nerd and used to spend most of the time in library even during my school days. I was not much of a sports player back in those days and the same applied even today. My class had just begun for a week and I was getting used to the class which included my batch mates as well my teachers. I originally came from Kolkata and well I had a few Bengali friends here in the classroom too. I had also started to make new friends from all across India too. The campus life during the day was as usual but the real change happened during the evening and late night.

My classes had just got over and I went back to my hostel room. I did not know much about my new class but there was an ice breaking session planned right after the class. We were all supposed to meet at a shack which was set up just about a kilometre away from the campus. The timing for the event was set up at around 7:30 P.M. The entire batch of 45 people had gathered around the field and we were all pretty excited about this. It all starts from beyond the classroom they say and I was also very excited about this unofficial meet. We had all got ourselves ready and prepared to leave at around 7 P.M. Not a single person was left behind from my class and I had no idea that this party was just the beginning of a ball rolling towards somewhere very significant. It was me, Akash, Rishabh, Vaishali, Sayani, Neha, Naren (my hostel roommate) who were in one group. The groups were supposed to assemble and then move to Junkyard Café. In a quiet place where our campus was located this was one of the coolest places, we knew that most of the people partied. However, there was more to it that we could come to know later and probably, I can take a bit of credit to that. We reached the place and it was a Thursday with a lot of buzzing crowd already in and more people coming in already.

The party had started and there was already quite a buzz all around. Everybody seemed to be getting into a fine mood. The music was on and the drinks started flowing. I did not want to be the conventional guy who does not drink and being the "good" guy in this generation. Well, yet here I was on the other hand caught in the morality of the middle-class family upbringing. Amidst all of this the party was in full swing and people started dispersing here and there. The music was loud and the entire crowd of my university literally seemed to be there. I could see that after 15 minutes except for Neha, Vaishali and me, I did not recall anybody being around the place from where we started drinking. I asked Neha and Vaishali if they wanted to venture out from the club and get some fresh air. They agreed as we started to get moving out the place. Well, it was definitely stuffy in there and as we started to move towards the main road there was a light breeze and some drops of rain had started to come in too. We were all excited as we started to walk down the road and move down towards the second café that was a few metres away. We were dancing a bit and as we moved up the road a bit the rain had started to pour down even more heavily. Many of the students had gone up ahead.

The rain had started to pick up pace as we moved here and there. I rushed off to the nearest shed. It was the backside of a café. The café we were looking to visit. The raindrops were smashing against the asbestos roof of the café. Amidst all of this I could hear a faint murmur and some people giggling. I felt that it was from my own class room listening to some of the voices. It felt like the voices of some people in my classroom I stood there for half an hour and I tried to peek inside the café. However, there was a barbed wire covering that side and I could not. My friends had called me precisely at that time. I left that spot and went towards the front gate from where we all entered the café. The crowd had moved in here as the entire area was muddy. We all sat down in the corner area which was close to the external shed. However, as I was about to sit down in the corner seat, I could see some marks which had gone into the garden area. The area was dark and nothing could be seen. I felt a bit of unease and was trying to figure out what exactly was going on. Then a part of my mind said that may be, I am assuming things so I just let it go. We spent around an hour in the café before deciding to leave.

As soon as we were about to leave, I decided to go towards the backside of the café. My friends started asking why I was looking to go over there. I did not have a definite answer for that as I kept following my guts. The passage was at the back was locked through the gate behind which was standing during the rains. The entry was closed and I asked the café owners what was behind that gate. They said there was nothing except for the open fields. However, I was really sure that there was something behind the café. I asked them that can the gate be opened. They said that the gates are closed and have been closed for a long time. I insisted it to be opened as the café owners refused. My friends were also getting angry about me being so stubborn to go the back. I did not answer them but then I decided I had to take the onus on my own. I came out reluctantly along with my friends but I had decided what I wanted to do. As soon as I came out of the café, I asked my group whether they trusted in me. My group was confused for a while but then after 5 minutes they said, fine. I said to them form a circle and then form a hand ladder. There were 5 of us including me and my friends who were just standing there dumbfounded and shocked surely.

Another brick in the wall

I insisted and told them to trust my instincts. Although reluctant in the beginning they finally agreed. The ground was still slippery. All of them joined in a circle as I climbed up with my white sneakers on. I barely could move beyond the wall when one of the café owners saw me. As soon as he was about to ask me where I was headed, I jumped over the wall. The café people started to shout and my friends were all surrounded. However, I knew that I had taken this risk based on a hunch. I stepped into the mud and then started walking until I found that the ground was muddy. I just switched on the phone torch where I could see a few drag marks and as soon as I went up to a few metres ahead, I saw some drag marks apart from a body lying ahead. I was struck for a while when I could hear people trying to open up the locked partition door. I turned the girl around and there she was from our very own batch, It was Dhruvani, as she lay there unconscious. She had bite marks all over her body and there was a bit of blood oozing out from her nose. Finally, I could hear the door partition open up as three café workers along with the café owners and my friends started to charge towards me until they realized it was slippery ground and approached me slowly instead.

I took her in my arms. She needed immediate medical assistance. I was definitely not the strongest physically but my friends and the café people had suddenly started to pip in into helping her move to the campus medical centre. The ambulance was called for. My friends said to me that you really did manage to pull this off. I did not know whether they were giving me a backhanded compliment or not. However, that was not the most important concern. The police too had been already called on the scene. Dhruvani looked really weak as Vaishali, Sayani and Roosha along with me, Naren and Nini were asked questions by the University campus police station. As expected, I was asked the greatest number of questions that how did I get to know that there was somebody lying in the field? Who were the last people I saw if any ahead? I told the police that she was with friends which included my classmates. Well, I personally knew a few of them who did not get well with me or my close friends. Now if I assumed that they would have been behind all of this, it would be probably a bit more presumptuous. Anyways we were let go as we arrived at the hostel. The hospital campus was near to our hostel which made it easier for us to visit Dhruvani right after we freshened up. It was later in the night and the next morning we had early classes.

The six of us visited her cabin and saw her lying with the usual drip and other medical support system. I left the cabin and went to meet the resident doctor. The doctor told me that the drugs had been pumped out of her system. She was given a spiked drink which had MDMA and Cocaine mixed. I asked the doctor whether she could tell me more about any further issues that Dhruvani had faced. The doctor said she could not divulge much details. I probed her a bit further but she refused to answer any further. I knew I had to get the file and get more details of the case. However, it needed careful planning. My other friends asked me where I was and I just replied back with a smile. I knew that there would be a shift change at morning 6:30-7:00 A.M. before our classes begin at 8:30. This was my best chance and I had to take it. So, I decided that I would sneak in by 6:15 and wait at the corridor. That's exactly what I did as I reached the corridor at around 6:15 A.M. and took a machine coffee. After taking some sips from the hot coffee I did see the doctor leaving. The chamber was in the extreme left corner and the nurses and wards were busy with shift change. The doctor probably was too tired to notice me anyways as I made a rush for the records shelf of doctor.

I managed to find the file on the third row. I knew time was key and I went through the file where I saw the file mentioning physical assault and attempt to rape. I had a hunch that there was something more than was being presented. The police had also not taken serious cognizance of this matter. Anyways as soon as my file checking was over, I scooted from over there. I had my classes but my mind could not focus on the classes. My mind was going over that how the events had exactly panned out and how did Dhruvani end up being there in the mud behind the café. After all of that, I decided to go right after the classes to the area from where she was recovered. The only problem was that it was day time and therefore I could not do any kind of stupid heroics of last night. I had to take the help of the cafe owners. So, I decided to visit the café and although I knew that there would be police patrol, I had to find a way to move ahead. As expected, there was a police patrol near the café. Therefore, the way for me was to coax both the café people and probably bypass the police which was near to impossible. Anyways, I had to try which is why I went to the café around 1 P.M. in the afternoon. The place looked so desolate completely different from yesterday.

I walked up to the café and decided to ask the café owners certain questions. I knew that I had already collected a few foot prints on my cell-phone. However, it was time that I got some information which probably could help me to answer questions which the university and the police should have been involved with. Surprisingly even my friends had kept absolute quiet on this. Anyways, finally I decided to walk to the café owners. There was the manager who herself had been a student of the university. I asked her by showing the picture of Dhruvani that whether she had seen her yesterday late night. She said that she was there till 8:00 P.M. and then she left. However, she had heard about the incident. I realized that may be if I keep pushing a bit more information could be on the way. That is why I asked her if she could help me with finding someone who could give me some information. She replied that it is under police jurisdiction and she did not want any further controversy related to this issue. However, I knew that I can use her to get more information on this. After a bit of coaxing, Harleen, the owner of the café said there was Rajesh with whom I can get five minutes. He was there around the time the incident happened and he may be able to provide some information. However, it should not be more than five minutes discussion.

So finally, I got to meet Rajesh as he was just getting into the uniform for the duty. I asked him that can he provide me some information on the incident yesterday. He said that he saw Dhruvani come in with some boys at around 11 P.M. I took out my phone and showed my class group picture. Rajesh told me that he did not recognize anyone from the picture. I was starting to get confused but I knew giving up was not on the option. I asked him that if he heard any name being called out. He said that he would not be able to recall too much. I asked him if he could think of anything in particular. He thought for a while and then he said that he remembered two of them wearing an orange t-shirt and the one had red shoes. I knew these details would be useless unless I got a name or something which I can match on my own. I asked him specifically that did he notice anything about the shoes. He said he just noticed them because they were obnoxiously red in colour. All of this did not make much of a sense until Rajesh told me that some guy named Vipul offered him a 500 rupee note and asked them if they could go to the field behind the café the road for which could be accessed through the kitchen area. Generally, this should have been the first upcoming news.

Now things started to fall in place. Although Vipul immediately did not strike something sensation, I asked that how did he look. He said that he did not look anything out of the ordinary but probably he was sitting next to someone named Rahul. Bingo! Finally, I was getting information that made sense. So, in reality Rajesh actually could give much more information than what I was being made to believe. It had been already more than 10 minutes and I had taken down his number. The name Rahul can now help me to connect the missing dots. He was friends with the particular group in my class with whom I had issues but I could not make it biased based on my personal experiences. Rahul was from the super senior batch and apparently the son of the local real estate contractor with strong political connections. The group with whom I had issues had Kartik, Jatin, Suriya Aslan. They were from big political connections. Even if it seemed cliched, I could not think beyond this group. I had to figure out how to reach out to Rahul. I could not take help from my friends, the local cops and neither university officials. The way was to utilize someone who can get in with them but time was key. I headed back to the university as I had to attend a few more classes before the weekend came up. Right after my last class, the local cops came up for interrogation.

Knock-Knock who is there?!

The local people asked a few basic questions, and no movement was really happening on the front where the actual deal was. There were no medical reports asked for. All the investigation seemed to be revolving around to suppress the incident. Meanwhile I had called up Kartik with whom I was on atleast speaking terms. He initially did not respond to the call but I coaxed him to come and meet me at the meeting point behind the new made cake shop. It was sultry and hot but well I caught up with Kartik. He was trying to avoid looking into the eye. I asked him around three questions. Who is Rahul? Was the drink spiked? Was he a part of the incident directly. Honestly it all seemed rhetorical but I was kind of hoping that Kartik would at least give me something to work on. He said he was there but he doesn't remember anything relating to their group. I realized that this was futile but while speaking to him, I got an idea! There were three CCTV cameras one at the café entrance, the one at the kitchen area which looked over the boundary area beyond where the incident happened. I knew the police would have surely checked these two footages and probably done something with that. However, while talking to Kartik, I realized that I saw them and the others standing near the first club where the cameras were there. That was far off from the incident but if I could get hold of the camera footage, I can probably get an idea of what went on from there. However, for that, I needed to get hold of the café where we first went. The name of the café was Happy Place. I knew the owner but now the question was would I get something from there. As the evening was about to begin, I went to the café. The owner was there and he was getting ready to get it running for the evening. I went up to him and asked if I can talk to him for a while. He was happy to help although he did not want to share the camera footage although he did allow me to see the camera footage. I looked closely for a 15-minute time frame and at the end of 5 minute I could see clearly that Rahul joined in the gang. As the end of the video was coming up at around 12-minute mark, I saw that Rahul moved away from the camera and when he comes back, he seemed to be putting back something in his pocket. This means I was probably speculating but I knew that the video footage would lead somewhere. As the video was about to end, I saw Rahul slipping the glass towards Dhruvani as she was already stuttering. I knew that I had to get this out and make it count. Going to the police was definitely not the option available.

Time was running out but there was only one option. Dhruvani had finally been discharged. I had got prima facie evidence which I needed to use as soon as I can. Dhruvani's parents were coming to the university campus to pick her up. The café owner did not want to give me the video footage until I had to convince him that if he does this his café would be there right in the business for being the saviour of a student. As soon as I got the video footage, I knew I did not have much time to waste. The gang members who were involved were nowhere to be seen but I knew this had to go out. I did not know that whether I was making the right choice but I decided anyways to go ahead. I had set up the projector and arranged a small screen where I first invited the head of the department, faculty members from all the departments, my batchmates and of course the parents of Dhruvani and she herself. I told my head of the department that she needed to be there. The rest of the faculty members were also marked in a mail which was marked urgent but the message did not seem to clarify what was the meeting all about. Probably the faculty members and the head of the department had already realized this. However most importantly Dhruvani's parents had been informed of what this meeting was all about in advance.

Everybody had gathered in the auditorium and there was my head of the department as well as all other faculty members. I had also got the permission to bring the café owner as I plugged in the video footage. The footage was played as all the faculty members observed it carefully. Dhruvani's parents were alarmed when they saw the video. Dhruvani started to cry as then I stopped the video but not before the entire video was played out. The faculty members and the head of the department asked me to stay back. Dhruvani and her parents were also asked to stay back. They asked me what did I intend to do with the video. Dhruvani's parents could not thank me enough and finally it was turn for Dhruvani to speak. The faculty members asked what did she wanted to do about this. She said that she wanted a public apology from all the people involved in that group. The faculty members requested me and the café owner not to get this video footage outside and delete it. The university also requested Dhruvani's parents not to escalate the matter further. I then came out with the medical reports which showed signs of physical assault. I also had my particular speculation that who could be the main person involved in this. Most likely Rahul. Dhruvani's parents said that they will go to the media and police for this incident. I knew I was in trouble although happy doing the right thing.

Corner of Marquis Street

The shack at the beach

It was not until Goa police discovered their bodies marked with the same symbol found on the drug packets that we could identify their bodies. Also, from the Noida apartment although the investigation team did not recover anything except for a picture pointing to the grainy picture in one of the cupboards which was full of dust and soot. Those leads were the only ones remaining which were probably turning cold until and unless the investigation could pinpoint the bodies, the drug haul with the lady in question here. I had been stationed as an informer in the Delhi area working along with the local police under the command of a man who was not really part of the operation. It was generally said that to be a successful investigative journalist one needed to let go of their families, careers and most importantly the risk of live. Here I was although being mollycoddled literally by police where I was trying to be an informer. I had been here for more than two months and in these two months, I had explored the North and South Campus of Delhi, the private universities in Delhi where I have mainly worked as cleaning staff, janitor, housekeeping whatever you may call me. I had been trained by the local narcotics department how to immerse myself in the student life, observe and collect information. It was on the job training but honestly, I had spent two weeks on each campus which was frustratingly ridiculous.

In these moving around here and there in the four months, I have definitely witnessed a lot of rooms, common rooms with weed spread around here and there. However, I did not have much access to other kinds of drugs the synthetic ones or the real narcotics one. Also, I had no idea what was going on with the women's wing. Things were looking a lot frustrating as I felt I was hardly being investigative and merely being pushed here and there. I did not find anything remotely interesting at JNU. I always had my premonitions about it. When it came to the matters of Delhi University at both of the campus initially, I did not find anything interesting or substantial. Although I did find something fishy at both of the campuses. Normally they had great food joints around to bite in but at particular corners of the food joints, I saw that particularly Thursdays there used to be leaflets left on tables at the left and the. right-hand corners in a particular pastry shop. This was on both the campuses and whenever I have looked at the pamphlets, they have been brightly coloured and there was a sequence of numbers hidden between the phone numbers. The pamphlets read if you are looking for relaxed meditation, Zumba classes call the numbers. At first go these pamphlets as well as the leaflets seemed pretty innocuous however by a twist of luck and some introspection, I found them to have more meaning.

I used to find these leaflets or pamphlets being stuck on the tables but could not fathom it initially that how were they left there. It took me around two months when one morning as I had just come back from the private university duty near Noida and was being placed back on investigation duty back at Delhi University North Campus. It was around 4:30 A.M. in the morning and I had been provided with a cleaner's uniform based on the duty shifts and the timings detail information which was already accessed that I was assigned to the science lab in the campus. There was a small lab which used to operated by the students in the extreme remote corner of the campus. Even in those early morning hours, I saw the lights of the lab being on as I was circling around the campus moonlighting as a cleaner and the rest you know. I tiptoed from the opposite building which had rows of classes. The corridor floors lights were which was clear but did not help in seeing from the third floor. I had got my cell phone and the zoom was not too bad. I tried to peak into the room from the third floor as the lab was in third floor on the opposite but the windows were small. The windows were slightly open and as soon as I zoomed in the phone camera, I could see the silhouettes of three people moving in and around lab.

Looking inside the camera lens

I had my camera on for about 15 minutes and after 5 minutes of the camera recording, I saw all three of them coming out with huge boxes. Some of them were colourful and seemed more like candy boxes, and the other box toppled over from where three packets dropped. I could not see properly but those seemed like small pastry boxes exactly like the ones available across any pastry shop and also the one found in this campus. Interestingly when I zoomed over the boxes there was a sequence of numbers on the boxes and bingo, they had the exact same symbols which had been found till date across different location. I was looking at a picture from a distance of around 100 metres but the picture quality came up well using my expensive phone gifted to me. Now I knew that I definitely had to follow this bunch as I saw them walking towards the back exit gate. There was a small truck waiting from where the driver came outside to meet the three. Interestingly I could see the driver clearly waiting outside the Tata Truck with a sweatshirt and a beanie. However, the mysterious three I was going after could not be found out. They were all wearing black oversized T shirts but one possibly seemed like a woman from the gait. All three of them had sneakers and I could follow them only till one point where I could get cover which was a building intersection.

The three of them walked towards the van and the driver quietly took the boxes and loaded them on to the back of the truck. Now the problem was that when it came to a vehicle, I did not have access to any. Neither was I very good using two wheelers something which I was not proud of. Being an investigative journalist requires knowing at least these things. All things said and done, I tried to note down the car plate number which I did. I could get the number but I was pretty sure that the number may be fake. I could think of only thing at that time to call my local protection detail. The police constable was there with me, I gave him a call. He was waiting at the front gate and was on his personal bike. I told him that I needed to follow someone. His name was Rajesh Darpan and he was the local constable who was working as my protection detail on order of Lawrence Sir. He was reluctant for a minute and then asked me that would it be wise to follow the truck without having any prior knowledge or backup. I insisted that we need to get going as this could lead us to something really big or major breakthrough. I immediately called up Lawrence Sir and told him that I was looking to chase the truck down and then gave the details of the three who were involved on the campus. Lawrence Sir immediately told me that he is going to ask Rajesh to follow the truck while I should keep following the three. I told him that I did not have access to any local transport and when it came to using vehicle. Lawrence Sir told me that where there is a will, there is a way. He asked me to follow those three who were walking away towards the left side of the gate which was the back exit. The sunlight was still an hour away from breaking light although the sky was becoming clear from the night time. I treaded carefully as I passed down the details of the truck and the number which was being followed by Rajesh. Lawrence Sir had also arranged a local S.I. number who was also there to assist me and I got the go ahead to call him at any time for any kind of assistance. I saw the three of them disperse in three different direction and all the three of them were on two wheelers. I could not come close enough to the gate but as soon as the truck left and the boxes were given to him just behind the car there were those three bikes. All of them were covered in sweatshirts and had face masks on. I could not see properly the bike numbers and taking a picture was difficult since the flash would be on and without flash the numbers would not be visible clearly.

Although I could quickly take down the numbers of two of the two wheelers which I noted down on my cell phone. I missed the third number but I felt that finally my moonlighting across the university campus may finally bear some light. In between the court hearing in Delhi and Mumbai had also been going on although I was not asked to come for further testimony as of now. 4 months had passed and the case that had started from my university seems to be flowing in a direction that was not expected. I mean, I was here working with police offer working to bust a gang of Narco-Terror while me being still a rookie and timid too on many occasions. I still was trying to fathom out that all of this was a part of the bigger destiny. I was lost in all of these thoughts as I slowly walked back to the main campus with the two numbers I had taken and called up the local S.I. Nimrad Singh. He was a young cop and had joined the force very recently. Lawrence Sir told me that his batchmate Zaeem Topiwala had trained him and that is how he had got hold of him. He was really appreciative of him probably hearing it from his friend. I had spoken to him three or four times as he was not regularly around but used to check on me. I knew that I could count on him for help as he seemed very enthusiastic, confident and eager to help. I felt like he could be more of my elder brother although as of now we were not that close. I called him up at around 7 A.M. in the morning and told him all the details of what had transpired and gave him the two numbers. He said that by today itself he will try to track down where these two numbers of the motor vehicles were registered if they were not fake. Possibly the numbers may be fake but I had passed the make of the bikes as well. Most importantly, I asked that without tracking down the number what else could we do. He said, that they could not immediately come down to the campus and search the premises as this will blow my cover and the big fishes will get alert. However, he said that if I could get a key and search the lab on my own then possibly something may be found. It would be difficult and tricky but this was the way for the backup plan in case the vehicle numbers did not add up. I was also waiting for some updates from Rajesh. My shift timing was about to be over and I had to sign out. I made sure that I used my fake identity name. It was done so that I could not be tracked by anyone and nothing official was there on record as Lawrence Sir got me off record.

Operation White Line

I returned to my quarters changing on the way back as I just lied down back at my room. While lying down, it may seem funny I was wondering about the series Breaking Bad. I don't know which one of the characters I would be. Probably Jesse Pinkman as I was lost in all of these thoughts as I dozed off for a while. I knew that I had a lot of work coming up especially since the lab thing had finally come to the fore. Now here there was one doubt in my mind that how come I could not figure out or someone else did. I was working around a few campuses here and there nevertheless which were marked out codenamed "**Operation White Line**". The name was decided by the NCB and I was told of the same by Lawrence Sir. I was actually off the books and as I mentioned before, for the last four months I was just moving around from one campus to another. In the wake of my investigative journalism, sometimes I was feeling that I had become more of a stooge. However, then the very next second I recalled that I was learning and rather being a rookie, I was learning the real field trick must say. I had been trained in information collection and as well as some basic hand to hand combat skills and observation methods. Although things were about to hit a different tangent as I just woke up startled with my cell phone ringing.

It was a call from Rajesh and he said that he had lot of important details to share. He said that he followed the truck and tried to keep as much distance as possible. The truck changed drivers three times one at Connaught Place, then from there it went to Kalkaji and then finally at Lodhi Gardens. There was something interesting to notice that every time the truck stopped, there were suitcases which were carried by the driver and carried away. He continued to say that he could not follow the other two except for the last person. He carried it to a salon which seemed a fancy one and after half an hour he came out and he finally left the bike at a parking area and then he took a metro and finally moved into a locality near Model Town. Finally, after half an hour he left for office, it seemed which I made sure by following him to a probable call centre located in Old Delhi named Rapid Solutions. I thanked Rajesh and said that you have covered the job that I have always wanted to do. Indeed, it was investigative procedure at its best and I could not be thankful. I knew that what I needed to next. I would have to take on the mantle from here and probably do some off campus investigative work that I have always aspired for even though the journalism aspect is yet to happen.

Just as soon I had disconnected the call from Rajesh, within 5 minutes of that I received one more call from Nimrad Singh that I was expecting. Delhi Police had followed those two numbers and they had both dropped off the radar at two different points. The first one dropped down at Rohini and the second one at Lajpat Nagar. The local police units had been alerted for the bike numbers and the cross verification from the RTO will verify whether the numbers are genuine or not. Although they had their faced covered and even if the numbers are not genuine, lookout for those two bikes operating around that area had been instructed. There may be hundreds of bikes but we had to start from somewhere. I was laying around and waiting for something really investigative to do. That was about to happen as in the next three hours those two bikes were on the way back towards the campus and I was asked to report back there as soon as possible. I was staying around 40 minutes away from the campus. I ditched the local detail this time and reached the campus. Lawrence Sir told me that I needed to actually observe the two of them every day if they were together and if they were separated pick on one. I had to put in my old disguise of a student and meander around the areas they were. I could not actually enter any classroom which was a big issue but well the operation needed to be covert. I had reached the campus and was on the look out for the two which was hard as I got informed that they had entered campus 10 minutes earlier and it was never an easy task to find the two amidst the crowd. All this said and done, I was wondering around the campus for sometime because I was still trying to figure out what could they bring, how could they bring it and if they actually had something interesting (read narcotics) then where did they distribute it. Everything said and done, I realized I had to get my local backup and I asked him to come over. He said he would be there in the next half an hour. It did seem childish and without proper planning but I had no other option but to continue. The guy who follows them here was asked to be at the gate, the second guy was asked to rush in and keep an eye on the parking spot. Last but not the least, I was looking to find out the right spots to look out for them at spots which were busy hangout places. It was later that I realized after an hour that I was looking for the wrong places. After helplessly wandering off here and there for an hour, I got a call Nimrad as he said that the bikes with the numbers mentioned were starting off from the parking space.

I quickly asked him that how many bikes were starting off. He said only one. I asked him to keep following him. The other bike was still there and I decided to ask him to follow the bike. He said that the person was wearing a cap and shades. I said whatever it may be just follow the bike. Now I had to make a choice that whether I should stay back on campus and if so, where? After a quick deliberation, I decided that I should head back towards the lab. The evening was about to be set and even if out of three one was on the way and the other one was not spotted, they must be somewhere around. I had a hunch that probably they waited till around the sunset to be around the campus. I was not sure that whether this hunch would actually work or not. However, I decided that instead of chasing around the campus, I would wait around near the lab on the north side of the campus. The lab usually closes by around 5:30 P.M. I knew that last time I had accidentally discovered the lab and it's going about it was in the morning. I knew that the chance for it to happen was at best a split chance but I was going with it. Lost amidst all these thoughts the evening had crossed by and I had nearly scoured the lab twice as well as the adjoining areas.

Bored past sunset

There was nothing as such really going on even way past the sunset as I started to get bored. I had probably dozed off as I found myself waiting near the corridor of the southern end. I quickly brought out my cell phone and found a couple of missed calls. One was from Nimrad ad I called him back and he said that it was very urgent but he could not get through to me. He said that the bike stopped at a coaching centre for kids and came out after 15 minutes. On asking Nimrad he said it was near Lajpat Nagar. I asked after that where did it go? He said that from there it went to two salons one near Sarojini Nagar and the other one at Rohini. It seemed that he was taking out small tiffin boxes and delivering it in the form of some kind of small packages. I was on the call that I saw I was receiving a call from Lawrence Sir and immediately I switched on to that call. He asked me what was the progress and latest updates. I gave him the brief but instead he surprised that the bike numbers on the three of them were fake numbers. I was not surprised that honestly, that he knew already what was I up to. He added further that however there was a camera footage from the Lajpat Nagar that can get them an ID to finally get a lead on the case.

I told him that I could not report immediately as I was going to around the campus but nothing really happened. I moved on to the lab with the door being locked and I was at the risk of being exposed by the CCTV cameras and my cover could be blown. I have had nothing to eat the entire day and before I forget to mention the second bike had disappeared which probably happened when I was looking out around the lab. Now the only option for me was to wait for an update from Lawrence Sir. It was around 6 A.M. the next morning and I was famished. I knew that the change of guards would happen around this time. The time I had spent around the campus had at least been effective in getting the idea of what kind of cameras were there around the campus and where. At least, my training helped me in that. It was around exactly 5:57 A.M. that I managed to come out of the gate. I was on my way outside as I wondering that what was I doing and where does the road end? It felt like that I was on this way too long. Lost amidst all of these thoughts I was wondering when I would get to see the video footage along with Nimrad. I just looked at my cell phone and I saw a small message from Lawrence Sir had written that there was something interesting that had come up. I was busy engrossed in the task when out of nowhere a white ambassador pulled up and before I could realize anything, I knew that I was in trouble. Three men came out of the car and pulled me in. The next thing I remember waking up in the warehouse somewhere. My phone was also taken away from me and I realized well things have surely taken a turn. I had no idea where I was, what time it was. Engrossed in all of these thoughts as I was staring at a wall that had the exact symbolic marks and a code on the extreme side of the north corner very close to my blind spot. I was just waiting out for someone to arrive and I was about to pass out because it was about to be nearly more than 20 hours since I have had something to eat. Finally, the door opened and I saw two guys in a mask come up with a plate. It had biriyani. My hands were tied in a zip and so were my legs. I mean that is so conventional. The hands were untied and I was literally so hungry that I just wanted to dive into the biriyani which I did. After having a few morsels just as soon as I was going for one more, I found a phone inside the biriyani with a number showing up. I was confused for a while then I picked up the call.

The voice was of a lady with a strange yet strong British accent. She told me in a queen's English accent that so have I heard that apparently the intelligence and police agencies being frustrated at not being able to catch me has got a rookie to uncover my operations. What a pity! Just so that you know all of your agencies could not get hold of me and you think you a boy out of nowhere would get me in the bag. I know that you were the one who got one of my boys in trouble with your adventures back at the university in Sonipat. He was after your life but I was the one that stopped him. I knew there would be much more cooking with you once you have hit the radar. It is because of you and your little adventure as well as the judicial custody offered, I had kept myself low. However, I feel appalled that you had taken me for granted. What did you think that you would get an Id on one of my operatives who had been operating in plain sight for the last 6 years.

An empire that I have built, would be taken away by a bunch of activists like your Reena and Lawrence with your rookie at the helm. Generally, I have always considered myself an extrovert but right now I was feeling drowsy. I was about to doze off when she continued and said that kid you have taken on more than you can chew. You have put everyone that are close to you at risk and then too for something that is neither worth your career nor on the records of the government. It is where my head was spinning and I realized that whatever I had in the name of Biriyani had something more added to it which had started to take effect on me. I was still looking at the numbers on the wall and I could not still find the meaning to any of the symbols which seemed arbitrary but the numbers had a kind of patten and sequence my gut feeling said. However, I was in the spin zone and as I was about to pass out, I could still hear her say a few more words. He said my name and then he asked one of his men to switch on the video of the phone. The video showed a house which as I was blacking out, could realize was my home. She said that do you recognize this and then came the picture of my parents as I could hear her say that what will happen to them. Just so that you know, you messed with the wrong hand boy and I feel pity for you. I will make sure to give you a quick death since you are so young and too much of pain during your death can latch on to your soul and linger on to the next birth if you believe in that sort of thing the boy from the corner of Marquis Street in Kolkata. I dropped near dead having passed out and landing on the floor.

Epitaph at Delta Beach

Vannakam Chennai

It has been 6 months since I visited Chennai being relocated by Reena Mam under whom I was initially placed. She had been kind enough to utilize her personal contacts to move me to Chennai. Till now I did not have had any issues here and I was working with the piece of my mind. I was working for a local Chennai English paper. I was working in the department of sports journalism and I was happy to cover the aspects of the sports and be away from what I left behind. Things were going well for me as I had slowly adjusted to the filter coffee, south Indian food and the craze for the movies. Then one day I received an anonymous call from an unknown number and without saying anything the call got disconnected. This trend continued for some time until one fine day when I was going to my office, I received a letter from Reena Mam asking me to meet her at a particular café. I was quite bemused and flummoxed that why did she send me a letter when all she had to do was send me an WhatsApp or merely a call. However as far as I had come to know her in the matter of a few months and her being supportive, I felt that there must be something very important that she had to discuss with me face to face. I was eager and anxious enough to meet her as well soon.

I reached the café near the marine drive and there was Reena Biju. She had a smile on her face as soon as she saw me. We sat down for lunch and then before I could utter a word, Reena Mam started to speak. She said that she wanted to tell me something very important. I smiled with a bit of pretense. She took out an envelope which contained a photocopy of the arrest warrant against the people that had threatened my life and also that of Rafiq. Three of them were arrested and when I read their names and as well from the area where they were arrested something struck me. I was in charge of the investigation assignment after a particular gang that was operating from Bandra and the charges they were arrested on seemed similar charges. Reena Mam read my mind and then she continued that the police team was also involved in this. It was with the help of Lawrence the police officer that we could nab these guys who was in charge of the attack on Rafiq and me. She continued and asked that with which people did I get into trouble with? I told her the story this time again but in details. She listened to me as the coffee and the pasta arrived. After taking a few bites, Reena Mam told me that the police have got one of the names I mentioned. He is said to be involved with influential people.

The discussion took on an interesting note as finally the names of the four students that were involved with the incident. Reena Mam surprised the wits out of me when she said the name of the girl that was involved in the entire incident. I had no idea how she got the information. Then she told me that it opened a pandora's box that opened up during the investigation. The girl's parents did not want to go into record and also warned against publishing anything. Only thing, I knew that I was caught in the middle of the storm for a long time and I had been moving from one city to another. She told me that the police were now trying to find out that how and on what charges could the accused be charged with. However, the charge sheet was being prepared by Mumbai Police. However, the local Haryana police was giving the accused protection especially the bug fish who was behind all the incidents happening in Mumbai. Everything seemed a tad repetitive but it was slowly falling into place that where did I stand and what was the way forward for me. It is where the doubts that I had in my mind could be cleared. Reena Mam told me that I had to continue lying low but as soon as she gets an update from the Mumbai police and officer Lawrence the next steps would be ready. Amidst all of this I asked how was Rafiq doing?

Boom and investigative journalism

He was in his village for about three months and then he had re-joined although he was working from his home. His marriage had been fixed and his parents were worried for him so he was asked to stay back at his place. All that said and done, the pasta and coffee lunch done it was time that Reena Mam said hold still and we will meet soon enough. Now I was not so sure what to honestly wait for. Anyways I knew that despite the heat, the traffic and the food, I was still safe hiding like a timid guy despite aspiring to be an investigative journalist. Lost amidst all of the thoughts, I staggered back to my office. Reena Mam was on her assignment off to Madurai for a new Tamil movie production. Although it did seem that she was now more on the investigative prowl than what I could have ever conjure in my limited time on the job and may be misplaced adventures if I can call that. The idea for me was to get my head back into my job and move away from all the commotion that had been chasing my life. However, things were about to take a turn in a month or two which I would later come to realize once I received a court summon at Delhi followed by a special court of Mumbai. Things got really tricky here as the situation seemed to be going somewhere very different from origin.

The court summons that came for me were a week apart for me. The first one was at Delhi where the case has been transferred from Haryana to Delhi under special act for women related offenses. I had taken a flight early in the morning and thankfully it was a direct flight. I reached around 11 A.M. and I could not be more careful as I knew that there was more at play. I had informed Reena Mam that I was out for Delhi. She said for me to be careful and like before in Mumbai, I was again assigned a protection detail based on the witness protection protocol. There was two Delhi police constable out there right outside the airport and I was picked up and taken straight to the court. Felt like a VIP but I knew that there was more at stake there. We reached the courthouse just 15 minutes before hearing. My heart skipped a beat once I reached the courthouse. All of the concerned parties were present including the gang that were prime accused. Also, Dhruvani and her parents were also there. I knew that I was in for a ride and thankfully for the public defendant and Reena Mam my present address was kept a secret. My parents were oblivious to the fact that I was in all of this mess. I was more scared to safeguard my present location and address before I realized that time for my testimony was knocking on door.

Dhruvani although was accorded a special permission where she would give her testimony behind closed doors. The rest of the gang was also present at the court. The hearing began and continued for the entire duration. There were arguments and counter arguments. The charges that were brought in against the gang was outrage of modesty, sexual assault, intention of rape. These were already understood that the charges would be filed as such. However, I knew that I needed to take care of myself in case the real party to this case turned hostile. Also, I knew that time was running out of my hands to actually play my part in getting the conviction of the accused. I had been only able to collect the camera recordings from the café, however the camera recordings were submitted on behalf of the evidence. It only showed that my class mates including the local MLA's son was also present at the café. The rest of the footage could not capture against the backdrop of the dark fields which was the backside of the café. The camera footage was grainy even when expanded except there was one scene where they could see she was being possibly pulled. I had to attend sessions for three days back-to-back and I was putting up in the local youth hostel arranged by the provisions of the court. After three days, the court said that the next session hearing would be in next month for an expedited hearing and judgement.

I had come back to Chennai and as soon as I came back, I called back Reena Mam and told her of all the latest happenings. She too told me that there have been some developments on the situation here. I was summoned as a witness to the case and I was not really required to give any testimony. As I was already privy to a case in Delhi which had witnesses from which one had connection to this case so I was asked to report here. I knew that my finances were tight and this frequent travelling was not helping me with my job either. Although it would be later that I would get to realize that being privy to the case in Mumbai would turn out to be a game changer for my career. Everything said and done, I reported at Mumbai High Court where after a long time, I came to meet one of the first person I had met in the city. The one who for no reason or fault of his own got involved in this case and may have had also lost his life. Rafiq was sitted on the left side of the court along with a constable as his security detail while I had taken the seat on the extreme right-hand side. The twist of fate or destiny whatever you may call it could not have been more surprising than what was going on with me. Let me first explain that story first.

A story beyond a story

I was already on the assignment trying to be a wannabe criminal reporter. Amidst all of that, I came to know about this gang that was operating around the Bandra area. They were tipped off by the officer Lawrence who was already on the lookout for the guys that attacked Rafiq. It just so happened that one of them who had been rounded up named Ismail was actually the local goon who was running low level narcotics operations around the west coast of India. The name Ismail brought along with him some other local ring members who were part of the planning that had attacked Rafiq. However, beyond all of that the drug ring was being linked to one of the members who was involved in the other case at Delhi involving my university. So, everything said and done I was the common factor in both these cases. I had been on the case for only 15 days but in that limited period of stint, I had managed to get one local informer who went off record to say that the drugs cartel was also involved in other kinds of activities that included prostitution, extortion etc. He said that there were some big fishes involved out of which the local MLA of the area, corporator and a real estate mogul's son was involved in the trade. The third figure in the schematics was the one that had pulled me closer to the case and connected both the incidents.

Yes, if you had been reading my story then you must have been wondering that my story has been floating here and there. However, that is how it has been. The judge read out the charges including drug trafficking, human trafficking as well as extortion etc. Along with the charges now it was probably becoming clear that why was Dhruvani targeted back at the university. In fact, there were reports of another 5-7 girls that were part of other departments who apparently had been sexually molested, assaulted and were later abused by a particular gang. Now it was probably becoming clear that who were involved in the gang. However surprisingly there was never any action taken by the university in those scenarios. Given the way, university and the local police wanted to brush aside the incident. I can probably give a pat on my back to force that issue till court. However, I knew that I had a greater role to play as I was thinking of all of these while the court proceedings were going on. Reena Mam, had asked me to meet in between along with officer Lawrence who was yet to arrive at the court as the presiding officer was supposed to join us at the café. However, what is life without a twist and a bit of drama. That is exactly what happened as the court proceedings ended. As soon as I came out of the court, I saw a group message of officer Lawrence and Reena Mam.

I was already eagerly waiting that what could be the possible reason behind the text and what kind of scoop I could get from them, Even, I was excited to share my experience at the court. I was with a police detail and they were ordered to shadow us. That is why the police constable did not seem very happy to accompany me. He however grudgingly agreed to follow me. Rafiq along with his constable was also going to join us as we both started from the court. Our security detail which was nothing more than one constable each also tagged us along as we both reached the Parsi café. The same café which was my last meeting point when I was in Mumbai. I could see Reena Mam on the left side of the café and as we were waiting, I could see the Royal Enfield of Lawrence Sir just pull up. Then of course amidst all of this the owner of the café with whom me and Lawrence Sir had met welcomed me. I introduced the rest. The police constables were sitting on the opposite side. Rafiq was keeping quiet as finally I was the one who asked him how he was. What he was up to? He seemed happy and he was excited to share his happy news of getting married to his cousin in two months' time. However now the real fruitful scoops started to come in once Reena Mam and Lawrence Sir introduced each other.

Lawrence Sir told us a news that got us shocked although not completely unique in India. He had received orders yesterday from his superiors that he was being reassigned to a new case. So, he had been removed from the case. He said that there was a powerful force at play who did not want him obviously to be prying on that case. All said and done, he had a slight wink in his eyes which I would later understand what would mean. Reena mam, in between brought out an interesting scoop that was connected with the case. She looked at me and said that whatever had happened at my university actually had one more person involved possibly which I and the others had not been able to see. She used her resources and found out that Delhi escort services circles had named a lady who went by her internet username Xotic. She was a middle-aged, well-spoken woman who had been constantly supplying young women, drugs and even occasional weapons around NCR. The local police had been off her for reasons well known in India. After the incident reported at my university and the slight noise made as well as my sniffing around pointing to me, Reena mam continued had ruffled a few feathers somewhere. That was very likely linked to this lady. Rafiq was calmly listening to all of this when I asked her that how come she was getting all this information and was it substantial information.

Pieces of information in a sea of maze

Reena Mam said that her colleague who was in the crime unit used to pass on the information. Looking at me, Reena Mam said that he was a part of the team when he left me and joined the crime reporting unit. He did not continue for long but once he left, I asked him on which assignment did he join? My colleague told me about the gang that was operating from Bandra and the reporting stint that they were on. Apparently, the gang that had been operating was tipped off by Mr. Lawrence. I was listening to all of this and was finding it quite bemusing. Then Lawrence Sir started to speak that he had been working on a case where he was working in coordination with Gujarat and Goa police. There was talk of finding one of the big ones especially since a large amount of meth and other narcotics substances was constantly being found. It was not unusual to occasionally find drugs on the west coast especially being backed by Pakistan. However, for a long time, due to the corruption in the local units as well as the participation of some big politicians, no one could or wanted to pinpoint who were the local couriers. Ultimately a few months back with the regular onslaught of drugs coming in there was an investigation team set up with a special task force and that's how things started to fall into place. The pieces started to come together slowly but steadily.

A month back there was this tip off that small trawlers were seen of Juhu sea beach which was loading something. The coast guard had alerted that the drop had already been made and was already moving towards a warehouse located around Bandra. The local police were not aware of the operation of our special task force, otherwise they would have definitely tipped off the local gang and the drop would have been postponed. In the early morning hours, the Special Task Force (S.T.F.) nabbed three of the members. It was quick and stealthy operation. The custody was taken over by S.T.F. where they were lodged in a special cell jointly operated by Narcotics Control Bureau, S.T.F. and National Investigation Agency. I was provided half an hour for the interrogation when I came to realize that one of them matched the description that was in relation to the stabbing case of Rafiq. All things said and done, the same guys did not take much to open up as they started to give out names including of a lady named Xotic who was operating a huge human trafficking, drug movement in the northern part of India especially Punjab, Haryana, Rajasthan, National Capital Region. She was operating with the local muscle up there and had huge contacts with influential people up there. In fact, she was also key to many terrors group funding being backed by Pakistan's ISI to fund her. She has also heavily invested in many front companies recently.

The STF had only been able to understand that she originally belonged from Goa. She had been under the radar and had been operating for quite some time. However exact details were hard to find by except that her origin was from Goa. The Goa police was alerted but there was hardly any sketch although there was a lead. The handlers who had been arrested had named two couriers who were code named Little and Jerry. These two were from Nigeria and these were their street names. One was pushing drug up in the north and the west and the other in the South, Central and Eastern region of India. A special unit was already being formed under me when I received a letter from the Ministry of Home Affairs that I was being promoted to the chief of the police training academy. Now it is well known that when one is sent to police training academy what that means. The STF was still operating but until and unless the leads were found it was like chasing a ghost. The only hope was that there is a capable officer who is good friends with me and he has asked me to secretly cooperate on this mission. Lawrence Sir said that he knew till now that Little and Jerry were two Nigerian students who were studying in a private institution in Delhi. A description was provided, and a sketch was made out which was sent out to the units all over.

Confused and Flummoxed

Lawrence Sir looked at me and asked that whether I was going to help him covertly in his undercover work. I was flummoxed for a bit and could not understand what he meant. He told me that he needed me to help him out on a very secretive mission. He then looked at Rafiq and asked him that what was he up to now a day? He replied that he was just working on his assignments as a local correspondent. Lawrence Sir looked at both of us and said, give me a week and I have an assignment for both of you. If you guys are in, let me know as in the meantime, I need to arrange a few things. He looked at Reena Mam and told her that I will keep you in the loop. Meanwhile let's keep mum on all of this. Having done and said all of that, we looked for the café owner our very own information source. He was there sitting in his desk surrounded by the jars of biscuits and cookies. The police constables were on the other side. We quickly exchanged a few goodbyes and waited for the next week to come in. It was decided that Lawrence Sir would connect with us in a week from now. My flight timing was next day morning as we all headed out for dinner near Bandra itself ironically. We wanted to part in a celebratory manner as we did not know when will we catch up next.

After dinner and gossip, it was time for us to return back. We all went back to our respective places. A week flew by and exactly at the juncture of the week passing by, I received a mail from Lawrence Sir regarding my assignment. The e-mail was neither too brief nor too long. It was a medium sized mail. The synopsis of the mail read that I had to float around the campuses of Delhi University including some other private universities over a period of 4 months to gather information. I was promised that I would be paid a stipend of 40000 per month apart from my accommodation and food which would be taken care. Also, a security detail of one constable and one sub-inspector would be there. I replied back that I would be love to be a part of it and asked about Rafiq. I did not receive a reply immediately and it was later that I would get to know what he was up to? However, let us get back to the present dealing as to what was going on and where did we stand? The idea was excellent for me as this was the perfect way for me to actually hone my investigative skills and may be jot down my experiences which I indeed did a few years later. However, this was definitely the experience that transformed me and pushed me towards how to be an investigative journalist honing my skills on the job.

I was sent my air ticket to fly over to Delhi and I was specifically given the details of my local contact who was supposed to be waiting for me at the airport. Amidst all of this, I was surprised that I have not faced any threat, neither have I felt that someone was shadowing me. I did not know whether, I was missing the trick or there was really nothing? Anyways I reached Delhi on a foggy morning in the month of September. My flight had reached on time and I was waiting for the man who was described to be waiting there for me. I was flummoxed initially not to see him but after waiting for 15 mins, finally I saw the man. He matched the description as I walked up to him. I asked him calmly that was he waiting for me saying my name. The guy had a wry smile on his face as he indeed nodded his head and he said he was. I told him that I was here. He told me that I had been asked to report to St. Stephen's Campus. He said once you settle down in your room kindly call the informed person and the rest of the instruction as follows. Beating the Delhi traffic, I reached St. Stephen's Campus as it was just around afternoon. The heat was bearable and there was a streak of sunlight peeping through the fog and the clouds as I reached my room.

J.N.U. Campus

The room was quaint and silent on the fringes of the mega city. Everything said and done, I received an unknown number with a text. It was written that don't text anything apart from this number. Also, I was asked to use telegram app for all messages. I was asked to call on that specific number from evening 6 p.m. to 8 p.m. The message read meet me at the campus café of JNU. I was bemused and surprised that why all of a sudden at JNU which anyways had always been at the eye of the storm but never for drug or narcotics related matters by any stretch of imagination. However why was I called at the café, I got to know once I visited Lawrence Sir. He was there sharp on time. I had a barrage of questions and before even I started to throw them at him, he replied back in a soft hushed voice "I know you have many queries but first listen to me". He brought out a bunch of pictures from an envelope which contained three pictures. Both of them Nigerians who looked young and was dead with Mozambique style shooting. That is three bullets targeting the head and the heart. Lawrence Sir said they were bodies of Nguelo Martwinde and Akiliezwa Yarogo. They were found dumped in a warehouse of Goa close to Anjuna beach. The third picture was interesting. It was of a woman standing next to an epitaph at Delta Beach.

There was something written half in English and half in Tulu language, Lawrence Sir said I asked him finally what did it all mean. He said that in the past one week a lot had happened. The narcotics control bureau, special task force as well as national investigation agency had explored the leads and all possible drug dealers and prostitution areas. There they had come to know a bit more about this mysterious lady named Xotic. Some information was received that she lived in Noida under the name of Ritika Goyal. We found her apartment location from a known associate who was our informer in one of Delhi's biggest red-light areas. She said that she had seen this woman who kept very simple but she was not a sex worker for sure. Every time there would be a fresh batch of young women who came in and the police activity supposedly would be high, she would arrive at this location. She would stay there for a week. She had been shadowed but every time she was supposed to have been located it turned out to be false. In fact, the local police whenever they have tried to arrest her on charges of human trafficking initially in the last three years, she had been backed by a barrage of lawyers who have got her bail from lower courts in no matter of time. However there has been a new twist in the recent times with the drug haul that was seized.

As soon as the drug haul was seized there was a particular kind of marker found on the packets. It was shaped in the form of a square with a circle in between and a sequence of numbers. The drug was actually found from a container ship that was coming in from Italy. It was marked for a warehouse in Bandra and then following a trail of leads finally it led to a colony in Delhi which housed African students. After a long search, the local police raided the homes of all the students. Finally, we did arrive at the house of the two of them which you can see in the pictures. They were both staying in north Delhi and were students of a private college in Delhi. From their rooms, we recovered a list of colleges and a hard drive that contained pictures of a lot of girls with their profile details. The folder was marked Batches for Madam Xotic. Everything said and done as we were coming out of the residential complex, a young woman who said she was the sister of Akiliezwa wanted to give out statements. We got her statement where she said that her brother used to work for drug trafficking at private parties including acting as a contact source for high end escorts. Her brother had gone to Goa last week but since then he was untraceable. She desperately needed help to find her brother and her brother's friend Nguelo as well immediately.

Parsi Cafe

The maximum city beckons

It had been four months since the incident at my university had happened. The university told me to continue classes from online mode as they cited risk to my life relating to the incidents. Meanwhile I had got a trainee reporter internship for a news portal known as Fire Arrow. The office was Mumbai and I was provided accommodation and food services along with a stipend of 25000. I was asked to come over and join in Mumbai. However before moving to Mumbai, I decided to spend some time in Baroda. I had a relative staying there and I decided to spend some time there. It was the month of April and the heat had just started to become unbearable. Although later I would realize that a different kind of heat would be coming over in my life. I came to Baroda and my parents were more than happy for me to send away from home. Probably they were reeling too from the impact and effect of how their nerdy son had turned out to be such a rebel. I knew that this was the beginning of the changing life story for me. I reached there at Baroda in the middle of April. The very first day, I forgot all about the controversies and the troubles I had in my university. I went out with my relatives near Genda Circle for an ice cream trip. However, that trip turned out to be more than a scoop of ice cream flavour.

I had my train in a week to Mumbai. My university authorities had told me that I did not know what trouble was I getting into. The four students who were in that group were expelled and one was suspended 6 months. I personally did glorious commendation from my friends and Dhruvani's family. I also did receive a university recommendation letter however as I had mentioned earlier, I was not allowed to continue being there on campus. My parents initially were disappointed in me but they did want to pursue the matter against the university. Now let's get back to the present times from where this saga of life was moving ahead. I did not I would be tailed but I did have a feel that things were definitely looking a bit suspicious and not so safe for me. I was near Genda circle where me and my family were there and I felt a bike had tailing me for a long time. I had noted the number and the last four numbers 9963. I knew, I had to track it down. However, before I jump to conclusions, I had to be sure that there was something actually going on. I went to Baroda dairy and did indeed saw the blue Pulsar bike with the number plate. The bike did follow me around till the restaurant where we had dinner and then left away just before we entered the alley for the complex where I was holed up at Baroda.

It was around the third day that I had been here with my relatives and I decided to look for the bike. I was not bad with computers and pulling out data from the transport database would not be that difficult. Well, I tried it first with Gujarat and then nothing came up. It took me over four hours to find that the bike number plate was fake. Felt like a complete blooper although I knew this could end up in a futile exercise. So, it did, although I could not just give up. I looked up the biggest bike garages in the city and called the biggest three. I got a time slot to go to three garages. The purpose was to know that which are the garages that had the best access to information. Although, whether I would get the information was never a surety. The idea was to know that where were the places that actually worked on bike paper forging, fake number plates or dealing in stolen bikes. At one point of time , I thought I was becoming Abhishek Bachchan chasing away Uday Chopra the dealer of fake bikes from the Bollywood hit flick franchise based on bikes known as Dhoom. Now coming back to the question in hand the entire afternoon was spent on visiting the three garages. The first one literally did not want to entertain me and the second one had no clue. However, the third one had certain things to add.

The garage was named High Automobile Services located close to the Baroda station. They said that there was a small work station which was located beyond platform 3. It is operated by two friends Hanif and Krishna who have some connections to local MLA. They generally had a strong network and it was risky to ask people about them. I had got the initial information that one can get to meet Krishna who used to run a local community club. It seemed a kind of idiotic idea to directly ask him if he could give the information on the bike number. However, I had to take the chance it would have to be done at the earliest. I decided to see if I could meet him. I was said by High Automobile

Services that the best chance was to meet him in the evening at around 8. So, I knew this was it and that is why I went ahead on planning to meet him. The club was close to a residential area and I asked the club people if Krishna was there. They asked me what was the purpose and I said I needed some help. After a brief pause, one of them replied that he will be here by 9. I waited for half an hour and then I saw a tall, dark lean man enter as everyone welcomed him by saying Krishna Bhai. After a point of time, I was asked to come and meet the man.

Krishna the charioteer

I met with Krishna as he was there close to the carrom board along with the four other members of the club. One of the members told him that I wanted to meet him for seeking a personal help. Krishna looked at me with a calm demeanour and then he asked me what do I actually want. I told him that I wanted to talk to him in private for a moment. The other members who were standing close to him shouted at me and said get done with the business quickly. Krishna looked at me and then said ok fine let me give you 5 minutes. He asked the door to be closed behind. I then started off by narrating the incidents of a bike tailing me with a fake number plate. I asked him if he could help me. He listened to me and then smiled. He said how long did I take to figure out that he could be the right person to come forward to for seeking information. I said four days. He then laughed out loud and said, I am impressed. He told me he could provide me information on this bike number right now as indeed he helped in getting that bike the fake number plate. He added that he remembers this clearly as it was a request from a very close friend. However, he is surprised to know that so much arrangement was done to keep a tab on a skinny short kid.

Krishna told me that he did appreciate my gut to come out here so he would give me a heads up. He told me that I was in wrong with the group of people. He said he cannot tell me exactly what happened me but he did get some information that what was the issue. Aslan and Rahul had come and personally met him in the past week. Well, I definitely knew that I was up against a bigger force at play. I didn't know back then whether to feel heroic or to feel scared. Krishna told me that I was on an uphill task and I better be prepared. Things would get tough including risk to my life. I did not know if he was being serious. Whatever it was, I decided to take off since I had already got the gist that I was up against something big and probably sinister for me. As I was just about to get up, Krishna told me that Aslan was the son of a real estate mogul and Rahul was the son of a corporator. It was not as if I did not know these facts but the way these facts were said to me was to make me feel threatened. I gave a wry smile back as I was offered some tea as the conversation ended beyond 5 minutes to 20 minutes. I was the one that opened the door as I could quite a lot of people waiting outside.

I came back to my place. I knew I had to call up a few people before things really got a bit tricky. I called up Dhruvani to check if she was keeping fine. She had been out of the university for a long time as she has been asked exactly like me to attend classes from outside the university. The role of the university here seemed always shady. However, I did not know that what I was up against. Finally, the day for my journey to Mumbai had finally arrived. I was supposed to go on a bus initially but then I decided to go via Ahmedabad using the Vande Bharat. It was a seven-hour train journey and I was excited to travel to Mumbai for the first time. I had a window seat and I reached around 15 minutes before the train was about to leave. I did not know what was going on in my mind but I definitely felt a kind of nervousness. The train had just started and I was already scanning around the compartment to figure out that whether someone was tailing me. I did not notice anyone and the train was already rolling on. I was hooked into my phone and after a point of time, the thought of someone following me around looked completely irrelevant to an extent. In fact, I had dozed off for a while until the tea and the snacks arrived when I woke up and saw something weird.

I saw that were already three people sitting right in front of me when even half an hour back last I remembered before I dozed off. The food was served and I was worrying that should I focus on relishing it and my journey. The three people who were sitting right in front of me started to talk amongst themselves. They were speaking amongst themselves which although I did not want to eavesdrop, I could not control myself. They were speaking of certain random things but in between the words Mumbai, power and influence were being definitely and attentively focused on these words. The snacks and tea were done and I tried to drown myself in the kindle book, I was reading. Mumbai was still three hours away and I wanted to keep my head clear and stop thinking of what could befall me. I started to focus on reading the book while my mind was probably wondering what could be the scenario once I reach Mumbai and how should I cope with this. Thinking about all of this and peeping in between my book on kindle and sneaking a glance here and there finally the train had reached Mumbai. It was time for getting my luggage in order which included a backpack near me and a trolley on the top luggage chamber. As I went forward to pick up the luggage trolley from the top shelf, I felt a slight shove and once I turned back there was no one.

CST

The train had finally reached CST. I was nervous and confused as I deboarded. I was told by my company to reach Malad west as per the address given to me. It was the company hostel where they said I could stay for my probation period. After that, I had to look for my own accommodation. I reached for a taxi but before that I spent around half an hour waiting for something to happen. At that time, I was literally cursing myself that why was I being so timid or being a coward. Is it just about the safety for myself or was I a part of doing something that had bigger implications. I did not want to get involved in further trouble but I already knew that I was already knee deep in issues where I did not have much control. So here the idea for me was to check in and wait to get onboard the company work so that atleast I can divert my mind from many of the useless paranoia attacks. Whatever it was, I boarded the taxi and was on my way to Malad west company hostel. I reached the building and made my way to fourth floor. Voila, it was like a normal housing complex room where I was greeted by a fellow journalist named Rafiq Ahmed. He was also a part of the same organization and had joined the company just a month back although a localite from the Juhu area.

I went out in the evening for a cup of the special Mumbai cutting chai. As I sat in the local tea shop and was having a chat with Rafiq. I looked from the corner of my eye that I was being tailed. I paid for the tea and started to take a walk with Rafiq. He took me near the office from where I was supposed to start working from tomorrow. I knew that a new chapter was supposed to begin from tomorrow. I was excited and tensed at the same time. Tomorrow morning, I would get to know what awaits me. After all of these thoughts and introspection I was just putting the cup back to the shopkeeper when suddenly I heard a shout. It was just a moment of change and I saw Rafiq being hit by a knife stab laying down on the kerb. Amidst all of this commotion the guy, I thought who was tailing me left with the beanie put down on his face as he sped off. I did not know what to do. Rafiq was bleeding from the stomach area as the locals arranged for him to be taken to the hospital. Everything considered, I kept calm but now I was tried to figure out that what have I done that a bunch of people were after my life. The questions would probably line up as I was about to find the answers with the time ahead. I waited for the answers.

Next morning before I went to my office, I had decided that I had to meet Rafiq. However, by this time, I knew that I had to take every step very carefully. Instead of trying to visit him in the hospital in the morning, I went to the hospital and stayed there. I had followed Rafiq half an hour later where he was admitted to a general ward cabin. He needed a huge amount of blood which was of O positive group. The arrangement of the blood was not easy but thanks to my blood donation card which I had with me; I could get him two blood bottles. At that time, it was the least I could do. However, I was still at that time worried that I may be targeted and may be the people were all involved at something bigger level. I stayed half awake at the corridor and somehow managed to get a cup noodle at the hospital canteen downstairs. I left at 8 A.M. in a taxi with a mix of paranoia and anxiety as I went to meet my office staff for the first time. The first one I had met because of me was already admitted in the hospital fighting for his life. I reached the office early in the morning. As soon as I had entered office, I knew that I was the one in the hot spot. Everyone was looking at me. I met my reporting boss and desk manager, Reena Biju. She was from Kerala and seemed a sharp young woman. She told me that she had already heard what had gone down with me. However, she added that if one wants to be in the field of journalism then one needs to walk the line no matter what arrives.

I was assigned to entertainment desk and I was asked to report with my desk supervisor Reena Biju for a new film promotion press meet. I was excited a bit as I was fond of movies and despite all the stress of the last day, I felt that this could be a getaway from all that had been going on. I was happy to get on board the first assignment as I tagged along. The press conference was at Jio World centre as I boarded the car with my immediate boss. In between, however I had got a welcome kit and a small cake welcoming me to the team. The idea of being in a movie promotion event as an official press reporter was exciting although not really a part of the investigative journalism that I had always aspired for. People may look into investigative journalism as life risking, some call it yellow journalism. However, the patience, determination and the bravery needed for this kind of journalism is what is needed in India although the risk is at all-time high. I have already started feeling the heat for a small investigative piece that I had conducted at my university.

The press conference began as we got the front row seats. My desk supervisor told me to just follow the lead. I was excited and nervous as my mind was already loaded with too many questions and happenings in my life. The press conference was a smooth affair after which we were taken to the location set for a promotional visit. I was enjoying the visit at R.K. studios. It was my first time visit and I seemed to be shedding a bit of tension at that time however things did not seem to be that easy. As soon as the visit got over all of the reporters were coming out, I felt a brush and before I could see I found a small note in lying in front of me. On it was written "You have messed with the wrong people, prepare for the worst". I had just finished reading it and came out of the studio when Reena Mam was asking me if everything was all right. She had hardly finished saying the sentence when a bullet grazed my left arm and one just missed the stomach. Even today, I shiver at the thought of writing it. Anyways just like it happened with Rafiq, there was commotion as I lay down in a pool of blood. Reena Mam seemed perplexed but thank god because of the police arrangements for the movie crew and stars, I was immediately taken from there and got admitted to the best nursing home in south Mumbai.

It took me a week to recover as I remember that on the fourth day, Mumbai police local officer-in-charge came to meet me. He said that he wanted to ask me a few questions. I was really weak and I had specifically asked my parents not to be informed. I told Reena Mam to tell my parents that my phone was given to a local repairing shop. Also, I told Mam to tell them that I was on a local assignment in rural Maharashtra and I would contact them back once I return. However, I always had the fear in my mind that may be my lies would be caught. Anyways, the local officer asked me a few specific questions of whether I have had trouble with anyone in the recent times? I did not comment on the incident back at my university. The police officer asked me if I could give a description of any one who had attacked me or Rafiq. I said, I do remember some details of the one who attacked Rafiq and also could say the four numbers of the number plate on the bike although, I knew that the number plate has the highest possibility of being fake. Mumbai police assured me that they would run a check on the number and as well the description based on the sketch. I was asked that I should take one more week to get back to work. However, I just could not lay low.

The sling and the shot

I had got my hands in a sling, and I reported back to the office after a week. The police patrol was given to me. I was provided with a constable and asked to report to the local Mumbai station every day. The day was overcast and started raining as I reached the office. I was sent a car by my office as the police constable accompanying me made me feel uncomfortable and conscious. The ride was for half an hour. Reena Mam was already waiting at the reception including other office members from all other departments including the Chief Editor. He was there as well as he welcomed me with a bouquet of flowers. He asked me which desk I wanted to be assigned for? I did not wait for a second and told that I wanted to get on the crime desk. Initially, Mr. Venkat Rao hesitated but then he asked me why do I want to join the crime branch, I said that I have always been inspired about taking risks. He said that he had no issues but for that department, I will not be able to work with Reena Mam. Although I was provided the freedom to choose to work on the assignment of my choice. I had decided to work on the assignment related to the current attacks on me and Rafiq. Mr, Rao looked at me with some confusion trying to determine whether I was serious or not and then he finally yielded.

He said that my organization would help me to get all the support needed for this case. Rafiq had also been released and he has gone back home in Lucknow. I was assigned to Lawrence Rinto who was originally a Goanese but belonged to Gujarat and worked in Mumbai crime journalism for the last 15 years. He would be my local guide and he also had local police resources contact. He was a young-looking tall man in the mid-forties. He had a friendly demeanour and he told me that if I was fit enough to move around, he would like me to take me around a place. However, before that he would like to meet the local police station where I was asked to report as well as the officer in charge. So, we got into the car of his as the local constable joined. We visited the station and meet local officer Kirti Parmar who was the officer-in-charge. Although short in height like me, he had the brightness in his eyes and a spark that seemed to showcase curiosity. He asked me how was I doing and then he said that they have run a background check on the bike number plate and as pretty much expected it was false. However, they have got a sketch based on the ideas of the description and he handed it over to me. Lawrence told me that he wanted to take me to a place near Church Gate station which was a local Parsi café . The café had been his favourite and famous joint for getting all the local news of the entire Mumbai city. It was owned by Kirtan Bhai Sodawala whose family had owned this café for the last 135 years. Lawrence Rinto took me there and got me introduced to the owner. He seemed a jolly middle-aged man with some elements as expected from a Gujarati Parsi man was there. He offered us his famous lemon cake with cups of his café special tea. Then he directly cut to the chase. He asked me that if I had ever got involved with anyone in the past. He asked me to be specific and not to leave out any details. I initially hesitated but then I started to open up and began to talk about the incident that I have had in my university. He asked me that can I provide some names to him. I did not know that whether I should go ahead but I did. I gave the names of all the five people who were involved and expelled from the University. Lawrence Rinto and Kirtan Bhai listened to my entire story. It took me around half an hour to forty minutes to give all the details. In between we had two more rounds of the fresh cream pastry and soda made in the café itself. All that being done, Kirtan bhai said he will get back with information by tomorrow evening itself at the café.

Let the curtains drop

I was asked to stay back at the guesthouse and there were local police posted out there. I don't know if that was supposed to give me comfort. Yet I was there with all the paranoia and anxiety. My mind kept wondering about Rafiq with whom I had a phone call. He was still bed ridden and his 19 stiches was healing and he would take another month to be back. In between the worries and the paranoia, anxiety the night was spent tossing around the bed and worrying about the slightest noise. The local constable slept in the bed right in the hallway. Most of the time, I was awake and then somehow, I managed to get past that night. I was more worried and excited to get the information at the Parsi café. As an aspiring crime as well as investigative journalist, I knew that I had to get around my own. I had an assignment lined up for my learning gig as an investigative journalist although my own demons were also chasing me. I was assigned to Harinder Sandhu. He is a Jat who was around 33-35 and seemed to be man that wanted to be on the field. I was asked to go with him and follow on a tip that revolved around a local smuggling ring around Andheri and Bandra. However, by around 5:30 P.M. I was also assigned to meet Kirtan Bhai Sodawala at Parsi café with the local officer-in-charge Lawrence also being there.

I reached the café at around 5:15 and was welcomed by Kirtan bhai. He offered me generously a cup of tea although he could probably a sense of anxiety and worry in my eyes. He told me to calm down. I sat down sipping on the cup of tea and in the next 10 minutes, I saw my local police associate saluting someone as I could see Lawrence Rinto get off board his Royal Enfield. So finally, we were all there as we sat down in the corner table. Kirtan Patel started looking straight at me and said, I was surely in trouble. He said that the people I had got involved in back at the university were from a local Jat family. The others involved there were from Hissar, Sohna and Rohtak respectively and all of them were local sarpanch. Inside information on at least two respondents also brought out an interesting information that some of them were involved with the smuggling of drugs from North India to the west coast and then delivering it to the east from where it is moved to other countries in the golden triangle. Now I was surprised as to how so much of diabolical information could be accessed by Kirtanbhai in such a short manner. Also how did these people end up being in university without being checked. Lawrence Rinto asked that what kind of influence and trouble could be expected from them. Kirtanbhai said looking at me straight cold possible murder.

He continued to tell me that the best option for me would be to move away from Mumbai to other part of India. I told them that what is the use of all of this? I could be chased down to any other part of the country. Kirtanbhai told me that well that could happen but most importantly my chances of survival in Mumbai was slim and also they had targeted me once here and the other time I got saved which are enough odds for me. He said I should start to look for areas much more remote. After listening to all of this, I seemed to be in so much of cognitive dissonance and felt like more of an escapist. However, I knew that I had to consider my options and be practical. Lawrence also said that at such a young age getting into trouble with the sharks in water was something not really expected and dangerous. However, what has happened has happened and the only way was now to think of the next best option. I knew if I moved from here, it would definitely mean saying goodbye to my investigative journalism career options goodbye for now and most importantly a coward in my conscience. However, life always has their own plan. The café was right on the opposite side of the marine drive and the sun was setting. I could see the golden glitter of the sun as the lights were coming up over Mumbai horizon.

About the Author

Mitrajit Biswas

Mitrajit Biswas is an author writing on stories related to historical fiction, crime, thriller as well as Geo-Politics. He is professionally an academician and researcher also having interest in sports and travel blogging.

www.ingramcontent.com/pod-product-compliance
Lightning Source LLC
LaVergne TN
LVHW041636070526
838199LV00052B/3390